Changing Materials
Mixing and Separating

Chris Oxlade

Heinemann Library
Chicago, Illinois

www.heinemannraintree.com
Visit our website to find out more information about Heinemann-Raintree books.

To order:
☎ Phone 888-454-2279
💻 Visit www.heinemannraintree.com to browse our catalog and order online.

© 2009 Heinemann Library
an imprint of Capstone Global Library, LLC
Chicago, Illinois

Customer Service: 888-454-2279

Visit our website at www.heinemannraintree.com

Edited by Charlotte Guillain and Rebecca Rissman
Designed by Ryan Frieson and Betsy Wernert
Original illustrations © Capstone Global Library Ltd.
Illustrated by Randy Schirz (p. 9)
Photo research by Elizabeth Alexander and Virginia Stroud-Lewis
Printed and bound in China

16 15 14
10 9 8 7 6 5 4 3

Library of Congress Cataloging-in-Publication Data
Oxlade, Chris.
  Mixing and separating / Chris Oxlade.
    p. cm. -- (Changing materials)
  Includes bibliographical references and index.
  ISBN 978-1-4329-3274-9 (hc) -- ISBN 978-1-4329-3279-4
(pb) 1. Mixing--Juvenile literature. 2. Mixtures--Juvenile
literature. 3. Separation (Technology)--Juvenile literature. I.
Title.
  QD541O962 2008
  541--dc22
                          2008055124

Acknowledgments

The author and publishers are grateful to the following for permission to reproduce copyright material: Alamy **pp. 6** (© Avril O'Reilly), **20** (© Phil Degginger), **22** (© Bon Appetit/ Wolfgang Usbeck), **24** (© Kirsty McLaren); Art Directors and Trip Photo Library **pp. 18 , 25** (Helene Rogers); © Capstone Global Library **pp. 4, 5** (MM Studios); © Capstone Publishers **pp. 26, 29** (Karon Dubke); Corbis **pp. 13** (© Fancy/Veer), **23** (© Bloomimage); Getty Images **pp. 11** (Photographer's Choice/Jeff Smith), **14** (Photographer's Choice/Peter Dazeley); iStockphoto **p. 16** (© Nicola Stratford); Photolibrary **p. 21** (Mikael Andersson/Nordic Photos); Science Photo Library **p. 27** (Alex Bartel); Shutterstock **pp. 7** (© pzAxe), **8** (© Timothy R. Nichols), **10** (© Farsad-Behzad Ghafarian), **12** (© bluehill), **15** (© Kevin Britland), **17** (© Mana Photo), **19** (© Andresr), **28** (© Ralf Beier).

Cover photograph of children painting reproduced with permission of Alamy/© Tetra Images.

Every effort has been made to contact copyright holders of material reproduced in this book. Any omissions will be rectified in subsequent printings if notice is given to the publisher.

All the Internet addresses (URLs) given in this book were valid at the time of going to press. However, due to the dynamic nature of the Internet, some addresses may have changed, or sites may have changed or ceased to exist since publication. While the author and Publishers regret any inconvenience this may cause readers, no responsibility for any such changes can be accepted by either the author or the Publishers.

Contents

Words appearing in the text in bold, **like this**, are explained in the glossary.

About Materials

Materials are all around us. Wood, plastic, and metal are all different types of materials. We make all sorts of things from different materials.

How many different materials can you see?

Which of these things are made from natural materials?

Some materials are **natural** materials.
We get them from the world around us.
Wood, clay, and water are natural materials.
Humans make other materials, such as plastic and glass.

5

Changing Materials

This toy is soft and changes shape easily.

Materials can change shape. We can heat up a material or cool it down, or stretch it or flatten it. Sometimes we change the **properties** of a material. The properties of a material include how it looks and feels.

We can change materials by mixing them together. When we mix them we make a new material called a **mixture**.

Here is a mixture of different colored building blocks.

Mixtures

A **mixture** is made up of two or more different materials mixed together. The materials have to be well mixed to make a true mixture.

This is a mixture of different types of beans.

A mixture can be made up of **solids**, **liquids**, and **gases**. Ice is an example of a solid, water is a liquid, and steam is a gas.

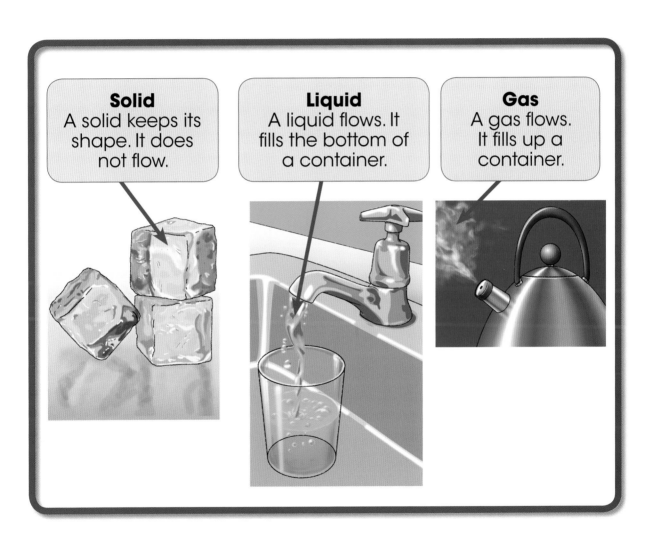

Solid
A solid keeps its shape. It does not flow.

Liquid
A liquid flows. It fills the bottom of a container.

Gas
A gas flows. It fills up a container.

Mixing Paints

You must stir well to mix up paint.

We use **mixtures** when we paint. Sometimes we mix water with powder to make paint. Sometimes we mix thick paint with water.

Mixing yellow and blue paint makes green paint.

We mix different colors of paint to make new colors. Two colors mixed together make a new color. When we mix we can make many colors from just a few colors.

Mixing in the Kitchen

We use lots of **mixtures** in the kitchen. We mix materials to make different dishes to eat. The materials we mix are called **ingredients**.

To make a cake, the ingredients you mix are flour, butter, sugar, and eggs.

When you make a smoothie, you are making a mixture.

A blender mixes ingredients to make a drink. A smoothie is a mixture of **liquid** juice, milk or yogurt, and tiny pieces of **solid** fruit.

Making New Materials

This girl is making a model from a material called papier mâché.

We can make new materials using **mixtures**. For example, papier mâché is a material made by mixing glue and paper. When the mixture dries, it changes. It gets hard.

When we make a new material by mixing, it can have different **properties** from the **ingredients** in the mixture. Concrete is made of cement powder, sand, and water. When it dries, the concrete mixture sets as hard as rock.

A concrete mixer mixes up the ingredients for concrete.

Dissolving

When we mix some materials with water, the materials seem to disappear. For example, when sugar is stirred into tea or coffee, the grains of sugar gradually get smaller until they are gone.

The grains of sugar will dissolve in the tea.

The sugar stirred into tea does not really disappear. Instead, it breaks up into tiny pieces and mixes with the water. The pieces are too small to see. This breaking up or change is called **dissolving**.

Seawater contains lots of dissolved salt, but you cannot see the salt.

Investigating Mixing

Some materials mix well with each other. When you stir them, they mix together and stay mixed. Try mixing a little milk and water together in a bowl. Do they mix easily?

Do milk and water stay mixed together?

Now try making some other **mixtures**.
Try these materials:

❋ salt and water

❋ flour and salt

❋ cooking oil and water

❋ sugar and water

❋ sugar and cooking oil

Do the materials mix easily? Do some materials **dissolve** in others? Are some hard to mix?

Write down your **observations** in a notebook.

19

Things That Do Not Mix

When you tried mixing materials on page 19, you may have found that some materials did not mix well. For example, cooking oil and water do not mix.

The oil and vinegar in this salad dressing soon **separate** again after mixing.

Wood does not dissolve in water.

In your tests, did some materials **dissolve** in water? Were there any that did not? Many materials, such as flour, oil, stone, and wood, do not dissolve in water.

Separating Mixtures

Draining a dumpling separates it from boiling water.

Sometimes we want to get back the different materials in a **mixture**. This is called **separating**. We can use a spoon with holes to separate vegetables from their cooking water.

Some mixtures are made up of tiny **solid** pieces of material mixed with a **liquid**. For example, muddy water is made up of pieces of soil mixed with water. We can separate these mixtures with a **filter**.

A coffee filter removes bits of coffee beans from the coffee.

Filters

We use a **filter** to **separate** a **mixture** of large pieces of one material and small pieces of another material. A filter has holes in it that small pieces can fall through. The large pieces stay in the filter.

This screen works as a filter. The soil falls through the holes in the screen. The larger rocks stay in the screen.

The water pours through the holes of the colander. The peas stay in the colander.

We can also use a filter to separate pieces of a **solid** material from a **liquid**. A kitchen colander is a type of filter.

Separating with Magnets

We can use **magnets** to **separate** a **mixture** of pieces of metal and other materials. The pieces of metal stick to the magnet. The other materials do not.

You can separate paper clips from a mixture of materials with a magnet.

Scrapyards use magnets to sort metals called iron and steel from other materials. A huge electric magnet picks out the iron and steel.

The magnet picks up iron and steel, but leaves other metals and plastics behind.

Separating Quiz

On this page is a list of **mixtures**. On the opposite page is a list of different ways to **separate** these materials.

Which way would you use to separate each mixture?

Mixtures

1) Soil and rocks

2) Peas and water

3) Coffee beans and coffee

4) Paper clips and paper

How would you separate peas and water?

Ways to separate materials

✳ use a colander

✳ use a **filter**

✳ use a **magnet**

✳ use a coffee filter

What would you use to separate soil and rocks?

Answers: 1) filter, 2) colander, 3) coffee filter, 4) magnet.

29

Glossary

dissolve break up into tiny pieces in water

filter material with tiny holes in it

gas material that flows and fills a space. Air is a gas.

ingredient material that is mixed to make a mixture

liquid material that flows and fills the bottom of a container. Water is a liquid.

magnet object that attracts iron and steel

mixture material made up of two or more other materials mixed together

natural something that is not made by people. It comes from animals, plants, or the rocks of the Earth.

observation looking at something carefully

property thing that tells us what a material is like, such as how it feels and looks

separate get back the ingredients in a mixture

solid material that stays in shape and does not flow. Wood is a solid.

Find Out More

Books

Bailey, Jacqui. *How Can Solids Be Changed?* Mankato, Minn.: Smart Apple Media, 2006.

Llewellyn, Claire. *Materials.* Mankato, Minn.: Cherrytree, 2005.

Oxlade, Chris. *Using Materials* series (*Coal, Cotton, Glass, Metal, Oil, Paper, Plastic, Rock, Rubber, Silk, Soil, Water, Wood, Wool*). Chicago: Heinemann Library, 2004–2005.

Oxlade, Chris. *Changing Materials.* New York: Crabtree, 2008.

Websites

www.crickweb.co.uk/assets/resources/flash.php?&file=materials

www.crickweb.co.uk/assets/resources/flash.php?&file=materials2d
Visit these web pages for interactive science activities.

Index